# Jay Cooper

# the SPY NEXT DOOR

## The Curse of the Mummy's Tummy

**SCHOLASTIC PRESS**
**NEW YORK**

For Henry and Annie:
friends, adversaries, siblings.

All rights reserved. Published by Scholastic Press, an imprint of Scholastic Inc., *Publishers since 1920.*
SCHOLASTIC, SCHOLASTIC PRESS, and associated logos are trademarks and/or registered trademarks of Scholastic Inc.

The publisher does not have any control over and does not assume any responsibility for author or third-party websites or their content.

Library of Congress Cataloging-in-Publication Data available

ISBN 978-0-545-93298-1

10 9 8 7 6 5 4 3 2 1                    17 18 19 20 21

Printed in the U.S.A.      23
First edition, September 2017

Book design by Nina Goffi

# CHAPTER 1

## Flags and Snags

It sure looked like the end for Dexter Drabner . . . the end of his game of Capture the Flag at recess, that is! Dex had to choose between surrendering his team's flag to Millicent, the world's biggest bully, or dropping to certain doom—and a skinned knee—six feet below!

Millicent yelled, "**WELL, DEX, WHAT'S IT GONNA BE?**"

Millicent yelled everything. She even yelled her whispers.

Just then, a voice quite close to Millicent's ear whispered, "Ahem. You've overlooked a *third* option!"

A leaping streak of pink whizzed past Millicent and plucked the flag out of her hand. Millicent lost her balance and tumbled from the jungle gym.

When the streak landed, Dex saw that it was one of his teammates, a girl that he barely knew named Aya. With a proud laugh, she waved the captured flag high in the air.

As Dex pulled himself to safety, his own flag still in hand, he realized something: **THEY HAD WON!**

The school bell rang, signaling an end to recess. Everyone ran back inside to gather their books.

Dexter caught up to Aya in the hallway on their way to class. "Holy guacamole," he said, smiling. "That was incredible! You must be really good at gymnastics!"

She did not return his smile. In fact, she barely seemed to notice that he was there.

Dex remembered that Aya was new to the school. In fact, she had only started at Kirby Richards Elementary a few short weeks ago. *She must be shy*, he thought.

Dex tried again. "Well, anyway, thanks. That was an awesome save. High-five!" He held his hand in the air.

Aya gazed at him coolly.

"I wasn't trying to save *you*. I was trying to win the game. Which I did. On my own."

Dex's smile wavered. "Yeah . . . sure. But you helped me, too. I was about to fall off that jungle gym!"

Aya stared at him. "Well, I didn't do it on purpose. I wouldn't have needed help in your place."

Dex thought that was a little rude. "It's polite to thank someone when they help you out. And it's polite to accept," he added testily.

Aya turned and walked away. "I wouldn't know. I've never needed help from anyone." She rounded the corner and was gone.

Dex watched her go, his hand still waiting for a high five that clearly wasn't coming.

# CHAPTER 2

## The Locker Beam

Dex walked to the library, fuming. "What a rotten tomato," he muttered to himself. Aya hadn't made any friends since coming to his school, and Dexter could understand why.

Of course, Dexter remembered, *his* best friend was a skateboard . . . But that was different.

Dex found the board hidden in a dark, rarely visited corner of the library. Why would a skateboard be in a library, you ask? The answer is simple: Dex's deck liked to read.

This wasn't just any old skateboard. It was a *Battery Operated Artificial Reasoning Device* (or B.O.A.R.D. for short). And the super smart supercomputer got really bored sitting in Dex's locker all day. It much preferred reading books in the library until the school day was finished.

"Come on, B.O.A.R.D. Time to get going," Dex said.

In the hallway, the pair ran into Principal Pickles, who was putting up a poster advertising the new mummy exhibit at the Girder City Art Museum.

Tomorrow, Dex's class was going on a field trip to see it. The entire city was excited about the mummy exhibit—the main attraction was a giant mummified pharaoh that was supposed to be *cursed*.

"You don't think the mummy is *really* cursed, do you, Ms. Pickles?" asked Dexter.

She laughed. "Cursed? That's silly. Mummies' curses are about as likely as giant mutant **RATS!!!**" She thought about what she had said. "Um, *less* likely, anyway. Now, if you'll excuse me, I've got to study up on my ancient Egyptian history for tomorrow! Toodles!"

From the farthest reaches of ancient Egypt

COME SEE

# HUN-GA-RE

Cursed mummified pharaoh!

Almost as soon as she was gone, B.O.A.R.D. began to ring like a telephone.

Dex made sure that no one was around to see them, then whispered to B.O.A.R.D. to answer the call.

A beam of light shot out of B.O.A.R.D.'s robotic eye. Up popped a hologram of a tough-looking girl wearing a tiny eye patch (or maybe she was a tiny girl, wearing a tough-looking eye patch!). Her name was Big K, and she was head of a spy network called the Super-Secret Spy Kids (Local Girder City Chapter). But at that moment, she looked too small to have such a big job.

"Hey! Why are you so big?" she demanded.

Dexter suppressed a giggle. "It's not me that's big. You're really small. You look like an action figure."

"Mr. McFur is going to hear about this! The holo-phone he installed in B.O.A.R.D. obviously still has some bugs." She sighed. "Dexter, I need you to come in for training today—I have another mission for you!"

You see, Dexter Drabner was no ordinary third grader. He *looked* like an ordinary third grader. He *acted* like an ordinary third grader. But beneath his ordinary exterior, he was *Agent SK8* of the Super-Secret Spy Kids. The fact that he was the *least* interesting third grader at Kirby Richards Elementary made him perfect for the job. You'd have to be crazy to suspect that Dexter Drabner was a superspy!!!

Dex's eyes lit up. "I'll be right there, boss!"

"Just push the button in your locker, rookie," she responded gruffly. "Big K out!" Nothing happened. She stood there, tapping her tiny foot impatiently. "That means turn off the holo-phone, B.O.A.R.D.!!!" The robotic skateboard bleeped apologetically and the tiny spymaster disappeared.

A mission! Dex's first and only mission had been to retrieve some stolen gamma broccoli from his former science teacher, Mr. McFur, and save the school from a monstrous rat. But that was weeks ago! He'd been waiting excitedly for another. "Okay, B.O.A.R.D. Time to get to work!"

Dexter grabbed the skateboard, glanced down the hallway, then quickly jumped inside his locker, and pulled the door shut tight behind them.

But Dexter couldn't have known that someone had seen everything . . .

The inside of Dexter's locker was a stink factory! The smell of unwashed gym clothes mixed with odors from rotten apples and moldy bologna sandwiches in old, gross lunch bags and the stench of muddy sneakers laced with skunk spray to create a perfect storm of funkiness.

It was also pretty cramped in there. Notebooks and old toys and the biggest dust bunnies ever known made it hard for Dexter to see anything. But eventually he managed to locate a mysterious button high on the wall of the locker. When he pushed it, a strange gadget stuck to the top of his locker began to hum loudly.

Dex had no idea what the weird contraption actually did. He had never used it before. He had simply been told that it would somehow secretly transport him to the Super-Secret Spy Kids top-secret hideout beneath Girder City.

Oddly, the louder the gadget hummed, the less stinky his locker became. The hum whirred louder and louder, making Dex's brain rattle in his head.

Just when the noise seemed to reach a deafening pitch, a blinding flash of light filled the locker. And in the next instant, both Dexter and B.O.A.R.D. had vanished into thin air!

The two reappeared at the Super-Secret Spy Kids' headquarters in a puff of stinky gray smoke. Dex and B.O.A.R.D. were shaken up by their trip—it took them a minute to realize that they had teleported to the secret lab of Dex's old science teacher, Mr. McFur.

FWUMP

SKATE
OR
SPY

16

Having your atoms scattered into thin air and then reassembled in a totally different place was a weird feeling. Dex felt a little sick to his stomach.

Mr. McFur stood at a control panel clapping happily. "Ha-ha!" he cried. "It worked! My newest invention, the Locker Beam™, is a success!"

"If you're so happy, then why are you crying?" asked Dex.

Mr. McFur wiped a few tears from his eyes. "Because, Dexter, the Locker Beam runs on *stink power*. All the gross smells from your locker were what brought you here. And I have to tell you, that is one **STINKY** locker!"

After losing his job as an elementary school science teacher in a spectacular rat-filled disaster, Mr. McFur had become the head scientist and inventor of the Super-Secret Spy Kids (Local Girder City Chapter). He was always coming up with crazy new inventions . . . each weirder than the last.

The sound of Big K stomping into the lab made them both turn. "There's no crying in the Spy Game!" she growled at the sight of Mr. McFur wiping away tears. Then she wrinkled her nose. "Phew! Who had onions for lunch . . . last week?"

Mr. McFur gave her a guilty grin. She rolled her eye and turned to Dex. "All right, Agent SK8. First training, then I'll brief you on the mission."

Dex followed Big K toward the Super-Secret Spy Kids' training facility. The hallway was lined with framed portraits of the most successful spies the world had ever known: Jamie Blonde, Mada Harry, and Dex's personal hero, Toby Falcon. It was a literal spy hall of fame.

B.O.A.R.D. stopped in front of a large portrait with a bronze plate on the frame that read SUPER-SECRET SCIENTIST M. The skateboard quietly lit a candle and placed it gently beneath the painting.

Super-Secret Scientist M

Super-Secret Scientist M was B.O.A.R.D.'s creator . . . and the closest thing he had to a dad! M had disappeared tragically one night years ago while working on a project that was so top secret that even Big K didn't know about it. All they had found the next morning was his shredded lab coat.

Big K's growl broke them out of their reverie. "I'm sorry. I didn't realize this was a tea party. Do we need scones? How about some doilies? Would doilies be nice?"

Dex patted B.O.A.R.D. on its head. "Come on, buddy, we've got work to do." B.O.A.R.D. sighed sadly and followed Dex down the hall.

Janie Blonde

Mada Harry

Toby Falcon

21

# CHAPTER 3

## Ready for R.E.C.E.S.S.

The training area of the complex was called the R.E.C.E.S.S. room. R.E.C.E.S.S. stood for *Readiness Exercises Covering Every Single Situation*. Dex and B.O.A.R.D. perched at one end of a long, looping metal track that ran the length of the room. Dex looked up and spotted Big K and Mr. McFur in the control booth high above them.

WIGGITY WACK

ROBOT 3

RAT 7

Squeaky squeak!

Rap Battle-Bot

R.E.C.E.S.S.
Control Room

FINISH!

GO  STOP

R.E.C.E.S.S.

Spiky
Ball Pit

Block!

Solo Robot
B-Ball Court

23

Big K's gruff voice blared over the loudspeakers, "All right, Agent SK8. This training session will test your speed and agility. The objective is simple. Skate from one end of the track to the other as fast as you can."

"Sounds pretty easy," Dex said.

Big K chuckled. "Just tell me when you're ready."

Dex kicked off hard and dropped into the quarter pipe. He was off like a rocket. "**READY!**" he yelled.

In the control room, Big K grinned wickedly as she pressed a button. "Release the *joysticks*!" she cried.

Half a dozen tiny black box-shaped robots popped out of hidden panels in the R.E.C.E.S.S. room. Each balanced on two tiny wheels. They shot toward Dex with uncanny speed.

They were gaining on Dexter, and it wasn't very long before a joystick got close enough to reach out with its stick-like appendage and *tickle him*! In fact, the tiny two-wheeled robot tickled Dex with such ferocity that he nearly fell off B.O.A.R.D.

"Ha-ha-ha! Stop it!" he cried. He kicked at the little thing. It went into a flying flip and broke into bits when it hit the floor.

Instantly, two more of the joysticks took its place! Their ticklish attack was so fast and furious that Dexter nearly peed his pants. These joysticks meant serious business—they intended to tickle Dex . . . *to death*!

CRASH!

"Dex!" Mr. McFur cried over the intercom. "Try the glue pads I installed in your uniform!"

Dex launched off a ramp and pressed a button on his elbow pad. Tiny globs of goo shot out with perfect aim.

"A direct hit!" called Mr. McFur from the control room. Three of the joysticks were covered in glue and stuck to the floor. They wouldn't be tickling anyone now.

Big K gave Mr. McFur an annoyed look. "Dex isn't out of the fire yet," she said. She flicked a switch. A ring of flames rose slowly out of the track ahead of Dex. He had a choice: jump straight through the middle . . . or become *spy toast*.

Glue
Pads

SPLAT!

SPLAT!

SPLAT!

SPLAT!

10

The last two joysticks caught up to Dexter. They revved up, leaned in, and tickled B.O.A.R.D. for all they were worth.

"**BZKKL!**" cried B.O.A.R.D. angrily. He *hated* it when people tickled him. A robotic metal arm shot out suddenly from its wheels and sent one of the joysticks flying.

The final joystick raced Dex side by side. Only one of them would make it through the ring of flames.

At the last minute, Dex gave the stick a wicked tail slash that sent it spiraling into the fire, where it squawked once and then disintegrated.

Dex leapt off a ramp and through the ring to the safety of the finish line beyond.

"Woo-hoo!" cried Mr. McFur as he and Big K joined Dexter in the training room.

"Nice work, Agent," Big K congratulated Dex. "Seems as though you're eager for another mission."

"You bet I am!" answered Dex excitedly.

"My sources tell me that your class is taking a field trip to the art museum tomorrow," said Big K.

"Yeah! We're going to see the mummy exhibit. It's supposed to be pretty cool."

"Well, it's apparently SO cool that someone has tried to break into it more than once!"

"What?" asked Mr. McFur and Dex simultaneously.

Big K held up that morning's copy of the *Ho-Hum Herald*. Dex read the story closely.

# HO-HUM HERALD
## BORING SINCE 1922

### NEW CAT SPOTTED IN GIRDER CITY!

A strange cat has Been spotted prowling aroUnd the GiRder City Art Museum at niGht. It's been seen yowLing on the roof, scrAtching at the back entRance, even slinking through the Egyptian wIng. ReportS of the cAT's breed vary. A locaL mini-mARt owner who noticed the feline had this to say:

PHOTO BY SQUEEGE

"Uh, I Guess it could havE been a tabby, or mayBe a black cat. I dunno. I mEan, it Was pretty dark. I really didn't pAy much attention. Hey, buddy, aRe you gonna buy somEthing or what?"

33

"The *Ho-Hum Herald*? You have got to be kidding me," said Dexter. "My parents read that paper. It's the most *boring* paper in the universe! I mean, their big scoop is about a new cat in the neighborhood? That's probably the lamest story ever!"

Big K gasped. "I will have you know that the *Ho-Hum Herald* is the periodical of choice among the spy set! It's supposed to look boring. Just like you. But the inside of this paper is quite remarkable! You just have to know how to decode the stories. This is information that even the news channels don't know about!"

"Who needs information about a cat?" Dex interrupted.

"This story isn't about a cat at all! It's about a cat **BURGLAR**," Big K growled. "One who wasn't spotted until that mummy exhibit was installed a month ago. Someone wants something from that exhibit very badly. And since you are going to see it tomorrow, I want you to be on the lookout for whatever it is this burglar may be after."

Fig. A: Ho-Hum Herald "cat"

Fig. B: Actual "cat": thief

*What could be so valuable?* Dex wondered. He pictured ancient tablets and jewel-encrusted statues. It was probably more amazing than he could possibly imagine!

He beamed happily at B.O.A.R.D. Finally, a new mission!

# MEANWHILE,

## IN A SECRET HIDEOUT . . .

A shadowy figure (who looked *remarkably* like the villainous stranger from our first adventure) flipped through a large book titled *The Big Book O' Egyptian Curses!*

He turned page after page as a number of robot henchman looked on expectantly. Finally, he found the page he was searching for.

THE BIG BOOK O' EGYPTIAN CURSES!

Official 1986 Edition

37

"A-ha! Yes! Here it is!" he cried out. "The Curse of the Pharaoh Hun-Ga-Re. It says here that whoever possesses Hun-Ga-Re's greatest treasure will have the power to *raise* and *control* the dead!" He rubbed his hands together excitedly. "Raising the dead. Oooh! That sounds like fun! Doesn't that sound like *fun*?" he asked one of the robots.

"But it doesn't indicate which of his treasures is the greatest! I wonder what it could possibly be? A 200-carat diamond, perhaps? A cursed sapphire ankh? I suppose we shall just have to see!"

The shadowy figure turned. Behind him stood a hundred more robot henchmen. And they weren't normal robot henchmen . . . they were N.E.R.T.s (Ninjas with Evil Robotic Tendencies)!

The shadowy figure addressed them, "Hear me, my N.E.R.T.s! Tomorrow you shall enter that museum and retrieve Hun-Ga-Re's *greatest treasure* (whatever it is!) and return it (and I'm totally curious what it might be) to me. Once I have it, I shall usher in a new world order!" He turned, threw his hands in the air, and began to laugh maniacally. "Mwah-ha-ha! **MWAH-HA-HA-HA-HA-HA -HA-HA-HA-HA**"—gasp—"**HA-HA-HA-HA-HA!!!**"— cough, cough—"Um, would one of you mind getting me a glass of water? Thanks *ever* so much."

39

EGYPTIAN MUMMIES

Girder City Art Museum

40

# CHAPTER 4

## Now Museum, Now You Don't

Principal Pickles was still bouncing the next day as the school bus pulled up to the art museum. She was so excited about the trip that she didn't even bother telling the students to quiet down when they got too rowdy. Through a storm of paper airplanes and spitballs, Dex's eyes kept returning to Aya, one row up. She stared out the window calmly, watching the museum with a serious expression. Just the sight of her made Dex fume.

When they had parked, Principal Pickles asked the students to leave all their belongings on the bus. Dex was stepping off the bus when Principal Pickles stopped him.

"Dex, when I said 'all belongings,' that meant your *skateboard*, too," she said with a smile.

"But . . . ," Dex began. What good reason could he have for wanting to bring a skateboard into an art museum? He climbed back onto the bus and sat B.O.A.R.D. down beside his book bag. As the other students filed off the bus, he whispered, "Sorry, buddy. I guess I'm going on this mission solo." He patted B.O.A.R.D. gently on the head.

"Bloo," B.O.A.R.D. replied sadly. As Dex turned away, he didn't notice the skateboard extending an arm from its wheel and placing a tiny sticker onto Dexter's back.

Stick!

Inside the museum, Principal Pickles led the class past giant ornate paintings and cool modernist sculptures to the wing of the museum that housed the Egyptian mummies. Dex noticed Aya studying an urn decorated with cats.

As they began to explore the exhibit, Principal Pickles told them the story of Hun-Ga-Re.

"Hun-Ga-Re ruled the ancient Egyptian region, Bur-Pe. He was powerful and very prosperous. In fact, Hun-Ga-Re was famous for being the fattest and richest of all Egyptian rulers. His appetite for power—and food—was legendary!"

**"I'M HUNGRIER THAN HUN-GA-RE**," Millicent grumbled.

Principal Pickles ignored her. "When the famed archaeologist Washington Wallis came across the lost ruins of Bur-Pe a few years ago, he was stunned by Hun-Ga-Re's enormous size. Despite the wrappings, the pharaoh seemed full of life. He even held a petrified sandwich in his hands for a late-night underworld snack!"

At the end of the hall stood a tall golden sarcophagus. Soft spotlights gave the golden tomb a strange glow. The mummy inside was huge—tall with a large, round protruding belly. An ancient submarine sandwich with a single bite taken out of it rested atop his immense gut, tightly encased by mummified arms for all eternity.

The students all gathered around Hun-Ga-Re to study him more closely. Dex had to admit, the mummy was pretty impressive, but also a little creepy.

Now Principal Pickles leaned in and spoke quietly. "There's something else about this mummy that makes him even more interesting. The archaeologist who unearthed Hun-Ga-Re found a curse written on the sarcophagus in ancient symbols called hieroglyphics. It translates to: *This hoagie can raise the dead! HANDS OFF!*"

YAWN!

47

**"PFFT. THAT'S HOGWASH!"** scoffed Millicent.

Principal Pickles arched an eyebrow. "Is it really? Washington Wallis never made it out of the tomb alive. They found his mummified body beside Hun-Ga-Re. The only clue to his tragic end was a warning he left on the dusty tomb floor in ketchup! It said, 'No, really! Leave the hoagie alone! Arrrghh!'"

The class was silent until Ms. Pickles giggled. "Of course, there's no such thing as curses. Come, students, let's go see the mummified rats!" She hopped away with the whole class in tow. Well, almost the whole class. One student was *missing*.

It was not until they had finished exploring the Mesopotamian wing and were about to head on to the rare collection of decorative Babylonian plant hangers that Dex noticed Aya was no longer with the group. "Um, Principal Pickles? I think we're missing a student . . ."

Ms. Principal Pickles looked around, shocked. "What?! Which one?"

"I don't see Aya."

Ms. Pickles gasped. "She must have gotten lost in one of the rooms. Can you run back and find her?"

"Sure!" said Dex.

The principal put a hand on his shoulder. "You can't go alone, though. You need a partner. Millicent, can you help?"

"**WHAAAT?**" Dex and Millicent said at the exact same time.

"No arguments. You both go find Aya. Catch up with us in the museum cafeteria for lunch."

Dex and Millicent gave each other angry looks that could have wiped out a civilization.

# CHAPTER 5

## The Hoagie Is Taken

Dex and Millicent found Aya right where they had left her: staring up at Hun-Ga-Re. She was concentrating harder than Dexter had ever seen a kid manage.

Without a word she started to climb onto the mummy.

"**HEY!**" Millicent called. "**GET OFFA THAT MUMMY, YOU LOONY BIRD!**"

"Go away!" Aya hissed. "This is none of your beeswax!"

Millicent stomped up to the mummy with a scowl on her face. "**WELL, MISSING LUNCH BECAUSE YOU'RE CRAZY IS MY BEESWAX, MISS FANCYPANTS!**"

That's when unexpected company arrived—three tall men in overcoats slipped into the room behind them.

*Uh-oh!* Dex thought. He didn't want to get in trouble! "Aya, please get down!" he whispered angrily. "You shouldn't be doing that!"

Aya had reached the hoagie by now. She turned around. "You don't understand! This sandwich is Hun-Ga-Re's greatest treasure! It has terrible powers! It can't fall into the wrong hands."

"Bzzt. Correct, child," one of the strangers in the overcoats said, his voice crackling and popping like static over a radio. "And we happen to have the perfectly wrong kind of hands for it to fall into! Bzzt!"

All at once, the three men threw off their disguises, and Dex's jaw dropped. They were robot ninjas!

"**FORGET LUNCH!**" Millicent yelled as she ran screaming into the ladies' room.

One of the robots wrenched the hoagie from the mummy's grasp.

Aya ran after it. "Drop that hoagie!" she yelled. While she was distracted, another of the ninjas shot a long robotic arm toward Aya.

Dex tackled her, knocking her out of harm's way just as the robot's hand came down with such force that it got stuck in the marble floor.

Hey!

Look out!

CRASH!

Then the three ninjas, one with hoagie in hand, took off through the open door.

Aya pushed Dex hard. "Get your hands off me!" she yelled at him.

Dex stood up. "Hey! I just saved your life!"

"That robot would have missed me." She looked at the doorway the ninjas had run through. "Now they have the Hoagie of Hun-Ga-Re!"

# THE HOAGIE!

Dex didn't understand. "It's just an old sandwich. What can they possibly do with a *sandwich*???"

"Fool!" Aya spat angrily. "Didn't you hear Principal Pickles's story? That hoagie is Hun-Ga-Re's greatest treasure! It can bring the dead back to life!" Aya turned and ran after the ninjas.

"But . . . that was just a silly story. There's no such thing as curses!" cried Dexter after her. *"It's just a hoagie!"*

The mummy room felt kind of spooky now that Dex was alone. As if on cue, something large and old began to rustle its bandages. Dexter turned around slowly.

Behind him the large mountain of bandages that was Hun-Ga-Re slowly extended his arms. He patted the place where the hoagie had once been, and found only clouds of dust.

Ever so slowly, he opened his huge saucer-like eyes and trained them on Dex. He took a mammoth step toward him that shook the room.

The mummy wasn't happy. He opened his gigantic mouth and roared.

Dex was hit with a huge blast of mummy breath! It reeked of ancient onions, long-rotten lettuce, and spoiled vinegar. The smell was even worse than Dex's locker!

The mummy lurched angrily toward him. Dex backed up until he was trapped against the wall. Hun-Ga-Re raised his gigantic fists and prepared to flatten Dexter into a pancake.

"**NO-O-O-O!**" Dexter screamed as the mummy's fists came crashing down!

But before Dex could become the newest installation of modern art in the museum, B.O.A.R.D. rocketed through the air, knocking Dex out of the way. Dex jumped on the skateboard, and together he and B.O.A.R.D. zipped away through the open door.

The mummy watched them go. He slowly turned to follow them. Hun-Ga-Re had to get his hoagie back!

# CHAPTER 6

## The Curse of Hun-Ga-Re

As Dexter skated through the museum, B.O.A.R.D. handed him his spy skating gear, piece by piece.

Strapping his helmet on, Dex said, "That was a close one! How'd you know I was in trouble, anyway?"

"Bleep!"

Dex peered around at the back of his shirt. He noticed a small sticker on his shirt featuring a tiny rapper. The big clock around his neck was chiming, and the tiny rapper was saying, "D-d-d-d-danger, yo! D-d-d-d-danger, yo!"

It was a *Homie Beacon*: a combination tracker and warning device Mr. McFur had invented.

"Cool! I'm glad you're here, buddy. We've got to find the stolen hoagie before that mummy goes on a rampage!"

D-d-d-d-danger, yo! D-d-d-d-danger, yo! D-d-d-d-danger, yo! D-d-d-d-danger, yo!

In another part of the museum, someone else was planning to retrieve the hoagie as well.

Aya trailed the three ninja robots, making sure to stay in the shadows. She knew what would happen if those ninjas got away with the sandwich, so she held up the small vial of nail polish that hung around her neck. Unscrewing it, she began to paint her nails. As she applied the polish, she whispered:

Let the cat inside me roar!

Aya examined her nails. She had painted them pink, but it was a strange pink that looked almost black. Even stranger, the fingernail polish began to glow.

Slowly, Aya's fingernails lengthened and sharpened into claws. A tail sprouted behind her and grew long and sinuous. Aya had transformed into the **PINK LYNX!**

She sniffed the air and picked up the ninjas' scent. With a growl she sprang into action. The Pink Lynx was on the hunt!

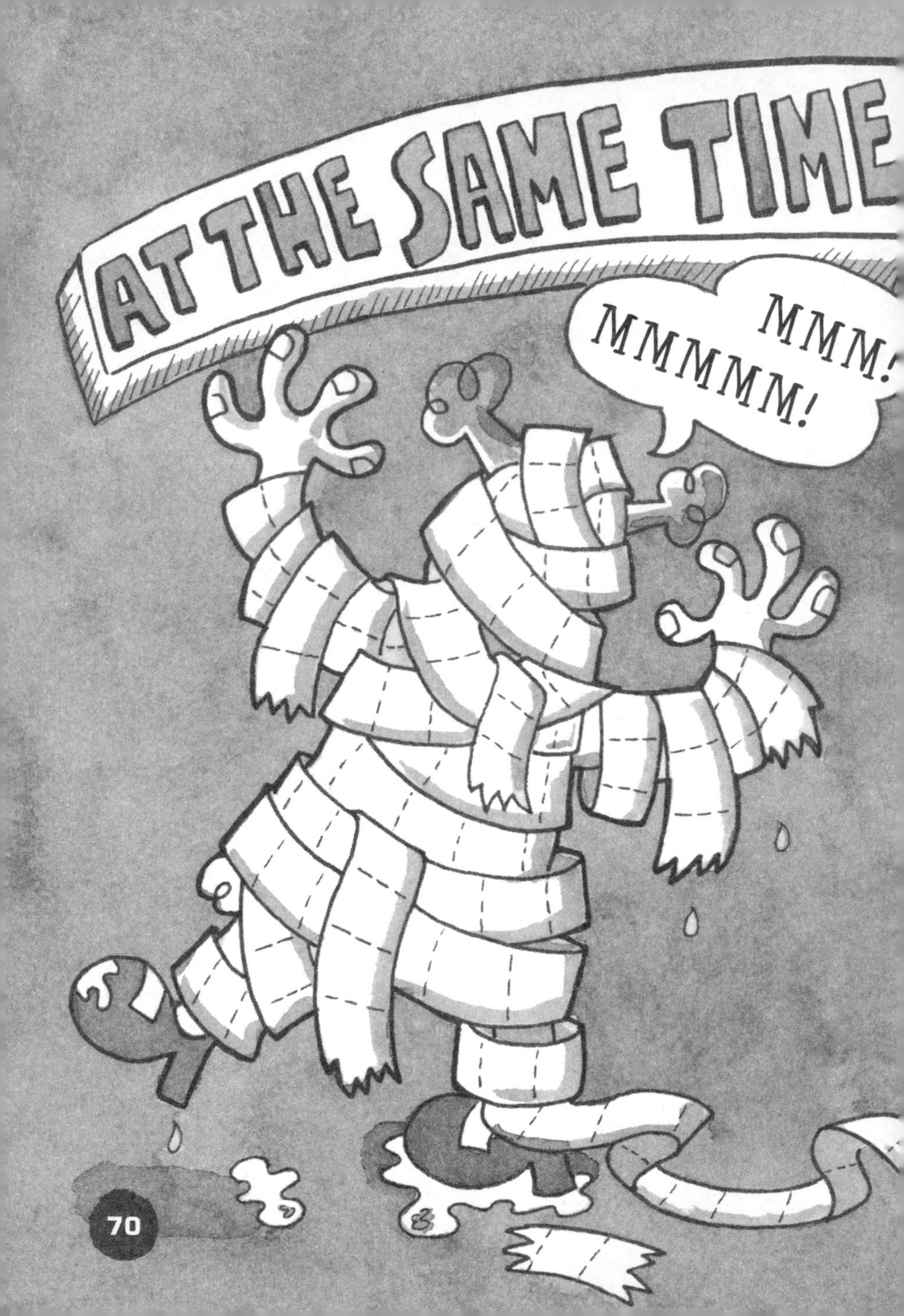
AT THE SAME TIME
MMM!
MMMMMM!

A woman was washing her hands in the museum bathroom when what looked like a monster straight from a bad movie lurched out of the bathroom stall behind her.

"**AAAAAH!!! A MUMMY!!!!**" the lady shrieked as she ran from the ladies' room.

Millicent couldn't see who was screaming or why. She'd leapt into the toilet stall to get away from the robot ninjas with such force that she'd toppled the paper dispenser and became completely entangled. Now she stumbled out of the bathroom and into the hallway, crying for help, which, because of the toilet paper covering her mouth, sounded like this: "**MMM! MMMMM!**"

The ninjas turned a corner into the wing of the museum that housed impressionist art. The pretty colors and blurry paint in the pictures lulled them into a trance until one of their wrists began to beep. A small video screen on his arm popped out.

The shadowy figure appeared. "Report, Number Three!"

"Bzzt. We are on our way to the meeting place. We have obtained the treasure!" the ninja responded. "Bzzt. It's a—"

The shadowy figure interrupted the N.E.R.T. "No, no, no! Don't *tell* me what it is! I want to be *surprised*!!!! Oooh, maybe it's a skull made of crystal. Or a magical scarab beetle!"

The screen lowered back into its robotic appendage, and the three ninja robots continued on their way.

They didn't see the large cat that stalked them, ready to pounce!

Dex had entered the Pre-Raphaelite wing of the museum. Paintings of long-haired, romantic women lined the walls. They lay in boats. They lounged on stone steps. They hung out of windows. They looked like they needed a nap.

In stark contrast to the painted loungers, things were getting crazy at the other end of the hall. The three ninjas spotted Dex and pulled out their throwing stars.

Dex didn't like the look of that, but he skated straight at them, anyway. He had to save that hoagie!

Just as he was about to grab the sandwich, a pink-and-black streak leapt past him, flipped in the air, grabbed the sub, and landed smoothly on all fours. Dex held his breath. It was a **CAT**. Or rather, it was a person in a cat **COSTUME**. This must be the cat burglar Big K had told him to watch out for!

**THIS WAS THE MISSION!**

"Give me that hoagie!" Dex cried.

"Bzzt! Give *us* that hoagie! Bzzt!" the ninjas cried.

"**HUN-GA-RE!!!!**" Everyone turned to look at the giant mummy Hun-Ga-Re, who had just lumbered into the room.

When they turned back around, the cat was gone. So was the hoagie.

Dex chased after the thief.

The ninjas chased after Dex.

And last but certainly not least, Hun-Ga-Re chased after them all.

# CHAPTER 7

## The Sandwich Hand Switch!

The game was on! Round and round the museum hall-ways, the unlikely group ran after one another. The hoagie switched hands, paws, and steel ninja claws.

Dex knew his spy mission was serious business, but he couldn't help feeling a rush of excitement. This was the most fun field trip he'd ever been on! (And the art wasn't bad, either.) He reminded himself that he had a job to do:

# SAVE THAT SANDWICH!

In this fast-paced match of foodie football, it was any-one's guess who would make off with the Hoagie of Hun-Ga-Re!

## The Pink Lynx has the hoagie!

**1.**

## Tackled!

**2.**

## The opposing team heads for the end zone!

**5.**

## Foul called for holding!

**6.**

## Dexter runs long!

**3.**

## Interception!

**4.**

## The Pink Lynx recovers the hoagie!

**7.**

**8.**

## The hoagie is in play!

**9.**

## Hun-Ga-Re takes possession!

**10.**

## B.O.A.R.D.'s heading for a touchdown!

**13.**

## Unnecessary roughness!

**14.**

## Distraction on the field!

**11.**

## An unexpected turnover!

**12.**

## It's anyone's game!

**15.**

## Who will take it all the way?

**16.**

# CHAPTER 8
## Secret Identities

The mysterious Pink Lynx and Agent SK8 faced off against each other, with the sandwich between them.

"Keep away from the hoagie!" snarled the Pink Lynx.

"Not so fast, thief!" growled Dexter.

"THIEF?!! How dare you!" roared the Pink Lynx. She sharpened her claws and leapt at Dexter with all her might.

Locked in battle, they fought over the hoagie until they were one giant ball of fury rolling around the room. At one point they even rolled right over B.O.A.R.D., who got tangled in the fray.

89

Their fight led them straight into Hun-Ga-Re's open sarcophagus. As the battle raged, the N.E.R.T.s popped up from behind the golden tomb and used their robot strength to slam the lid shut. The trio was trapped inside.

"Get off me!" Dexter grumpily yelled at the Pink Lynx.

"*Me* get off *you*? Ha! How about you stop stepping on my tail, Dexter!" she spat back at him.

*Wait a minute*, thought Dex. *That voice! I recognize that voice!*

"Aya? Is that *you*?" Dexter asked.

In the darkness, the Pink Lynx froze. "Maybe."

B.O.A.R.D.'s eye lit up as bright as a flashlight. It illuminated the interior of the sarcophagus. Dex stared at the Pink Lynx in shock.

The Pink Lynx shook her head. "Well, this is a little awkward."

B.O.A.R.D.'s light shone on the hieroglyphics carved into the walls of the coffin. "Bleep!" he said.

"What did your machine say?" asked Aya.

"He says that we're trapped in the tomb of Hun-Ga-Re. And he's my *friend*, not my machine."

"Pfft! The Pink Lynx doesn't need friends. The Pink Lynx doesn't need anyone!!!"

Aya stood and wedged her Lynx claws under the tight seal of the sarcophagus lid. Using all her strength, she tried to pry it open. When it didn't budge, she slumped to the ground.

"It's locked tight. I've failed. My mission is a failure!" Then, to Dex's surprise, she put her head in her paws and began to cry.

"Bzzkl Bleep!" said B.O.A.R.D.

"That means, 'Never say never,'" Dex translated. "B.O.A.R.D. and I have been in worse pickles than this!"

B.O.A.R.D.'s robotic arms extended from its wheels and set to work on releasing them from the stone prison.

93

Aya wiped her eyes. "You really think your skateboard can open the lid?"

Dex nodded. "I do. But first, I have some questions. How can a *sandwich* raise the dead? Why are you dressed like a cat? And how did you know who I was???"

Aya stood tall. "You may call me the Pink Lynx. I am an agent of an even *Superer*, even *Secreter* spy group than the Super-Secret Spy Kids. We are . . . the Spectrum of the Cat! I have been assigned with the task of acquiring the cursed hoagie and bringing it back to our headquarters for protection. And I was *this* close—until you stopped me!"

"*Me* stop *you*?" cried Dex. "I saved your life!"

B.O.A.R.D. bleeped angrily behind them.

Dex nodded. "You're right, B.O.A.R.D., fighting won't help our situation at all. Okay, so you're a secret agent. But how did you know that *I* was one, too?"

94

THE PINK LYNX

Super-Sharp Claws

Super-Sensitive Hearing

Cat-Like Smell (but doesn't smell like a cat!)

Magical Nail Polish Coats Aya in A STEALTHY Pink-Colored Costume

Climbing Skillz

Super-Agile and Flippy Feet

A Tail, Yo!

"Oh, that was easy." The Pink Lynx waved nonchalantly. "I saw you sneak into your locker. I waited about twenty minutes and opened it. It was child's play to figure out that you used a stink-power teleporter. No boy's locker smells that clean!"

"Okay. But how did you know about the cursed hoagie?"

"The Spectrum of the Cat has access to a secret book only few know of. It is called *The Big Book O' Egyptian Curses!* It tells of how Hun-Ga-Re had a wizard curse his single greatest treasure with the power to raise the dead! I've been trying to locate the treasure for weeks now, until your Principal Pickles hit upon the secret: **THE HOAGIE!!!**"

Aya sighed. "It seems I gave away the secret to those N.E.R.T.s at the worst possible moment," she said sadly.

Dex said, "Wow. So those ninjas—or whoever they work for—are going to be able to raise an army of the dead?"

The Pink Lynx nodded. "And if they can control the dead, they can control the **WORLD**! Now do you understand why it is so important to rescue that hoagie?"

"I do," said Dexter. "Listen, I know you think this is just your responsibility, but this may be one mission that the Pink Lynx could use some help on."

Aya considered this. "I guess you're right. Would you help me? I'm sorry I've been so mean. I'm really great with animals, but people are a little harder for me to understand."

Dex nodded. "It would be my honor, Pink Lynx. We all need a hand sometimes. And you can call me Agent SK8!"

B.O.A.R.D. let out a "Blip!" of agreement. There was a click as the skateboard located and pulled a secret lever that opened the sarcophagus. The large golden lid opened slowly with a deep, grinding sound.

"Great work, B.O.A.R.D.!" said Dex. "Now let's all go get that hoagie together! I just have one last question. What the hamhock is a N.E.R.T.?"

TEAM-UP HIGH 5!

WAG!

99

# CHAPTER 9
## Undead and Unfed

The Pink Lynx used her sharp cat sense of smell to locate the robot ninjas. The trail led to a large room in the museum that housed an ancient temple.

Aya, Dex, and B.O.A.R.D. crept quietly to the edge of a balcony overlooking the temple. What they saw gave them a shock—there weren't just three Ninjas with Evil Robotic Tendencies down there—there were hundreds! Dex looked worriedly at the Pink Lynx. They could fight three N.E.R.T.s, but taking on an army of them seemed impossible.

All the ninja robots chanted solemnly, their mechanical eyes locked on a marble altar that held the Hoagie of Hun-Ga-Re. A man in an Egyptian headdress stood behind the platform.

"That man in the headdress has to be their leader," said Dex. "I think B.O.A.R.D. and I should create a diversion, while you . . ."

He stopped midsentence. B.O.A.R.D. was gone.

"B.O.A.R.D.?" Dex whispered. "Where are you? Aya, did you see where . . ."

He stopped again. The Pink Lynx had disappeared as well. When he turned around to look for them, he saw that they were both held snugly in the grasp of giant mummy hands. Hun-Ga-Re had found them.

"Oh, sherbet," said Dex as the cursed mummy hands reached out for him, too.

Then everything went black.

When Dex awoke, he was tied to a stone column along with the Pink Lynx and B.O.A.R.D. Hun-Ga-Re stood guard.

Dex looked around. Dozens of ninjas had their angry robotic eyes trained on them. So did the man with the Egyptian headdress, who looked Dex up and down as he twirled his mustache evilly.

"So I finally get to meet the newest Super-Secret Spy Kid recruit. Agent SK8, I presume?"

Dex struggled against the rope that held him tight. "How do you know who I am?"

The man laughed. "Oh, I know lots of things I shouldn't! For instance, I know that you're the one who saved Girder City from that mutant rat not so long ago. I should, since I'm the one who gave your Mr. McFur the gamma broccoli to make his rat grow!"

He turned to Aya, "And as I live and breathe, the Pink Lynx! The Spectrum of the Cat has tussled with my N.E.R.T.s before! But no longer, I'm afraid."

Dex looked at the giant mummy standing impassively behind him. "Why isn't Hun-Ga-Re wringing your neck right now?"

Madstachio patted the mummy kindly. "I've convinced him I'm the wizard that cursed the sandwich for him all those eons ago. I told him I'm 'still alive' because it takes four thousand years to preserve pickles perfectly. Say *that* five times fast! As long as he thinks I'm the one who cursed his beloved sandwich, he's willing to let me near it. You think I'm wearing this headdress for fun? It clashes horribly with my mustache!" Madstachio leaned in close and whispered conspiratorially, "You know, he's not the brightest mummy I've ever met!"

Pickle Jar

"Don't do it, Madstachio!" Dexter pleaded with him. "That hoagie wasn't meant for mere mortals. The living should never control the dead!"

Madstachio laughed. "Well, of course. But, my boy, I am no mere mortal. I am Madstachio! And now, it's been fun, but if you'll excuse me, it's time for my lunch. One bite of this diabolical delicacy and I'll be the most powerful man on the planet." He paused. "I have to say, I'm still surprised that the treasure is an oversize sandwich! I was really hoping for a giant ruby eyeball. Oh well."

Dexter looked closely at the madman. He squinted so hard that the mustache almost disappeared. And then Dex realized something. Without the pharaoh hat and mustache, Madstachio looked just like . . . "Holy guacamole!" he whispered to B.O.A.R.D. "Madstachio is Super-Secret Scientist M!"

Dexter was right! B.O.A.R.D. let out a surprised series of bleeps and bloops. It was his long-lost creator!

Twirl!

"And now it's time for the greatest meal in history!" Madstachio said as he slowly lifted the hoagie toward his mouth.

Dex and Aya strained against the ropes, but it was no use—they were tied snugly to the column.

"Well, I guess this is it, B.O.A.R.D. You've been the best friend a kid could have," said Dex.

"Bleep bloo . . . ," B.O.A.R.D. agreed sadly.

The Pink Lynx said, "You know, I've never actually had friends before . . ."

"Better late than never, I guess." Dex smiled.

Aya smiled back, just as Madstachio took a bite of the hoagie that could raise the dead.

Then a couple of unexpected things happened at the same exact time.

First, there was a distinct cracking noise as all of Madstachio's teeth shattered.

Four thousand years held in Hun-Ga-Re's grasp had made the sandwich bread so incredibly stale that it was rock-hard and practically petrified.

Madstachio's mouth hurt. A lot. And he hadn't even gotten to eat the nasty thing.

Second, Millicent wandered into the temple completely wrapped in toilet paper.

"**MMM! MMMMM!**" She stumbled about blindly, bumping into the robot ninjas in her path.

Madstachio decided this mummy had to be part of a distraction planned by Agent SK8. **"GET HER!"** he roared at his robot lackeys.

The N.E.R.T.s circled Millicent, who kept asking if anyone had seen Principal Pickles. It sounded like this: **"MMMM! MMMM!"**

Someone else had noticed Millicent's entrance: the giant mummy Hun-Ga-Re. He became entranced by her mumbles. He was enamored with the way she tripped over her feet. He adored how she wobbled to and fro. She was like a small version of himself.

Yes, the most unexpected thing had occurred in that temple. Hun-Ga-Re had fallen in *love*.

The ninjas advanced on Millicent, their swords and knives ready for battle.

One of the swords poked her in the butt.

**"MMM!"** she said, which meant "OW!"

It was like a switch inside Hun-Ga-Re flipped on. With an earth-shaking roar, the giant mummy stepped off the altar, crushing one of the robot ninja beneath his feet.

Then Hun-Ga-Re let loose a roar so very loud that it shook the temple. In fact, it shook the entire museum. It was positively loud enough to wake the dead!

Waking the dead, it turns out, was *exactly* what Hun-Ga-Re had in mind.

Throughout the museum, the lifeless inhabitants of many exhibits awoke from their eternal slumber and began to seek out the master who called to them.

Most were mummies, but others joined the parade: There were suits of armor haunted by phantom knights, a smattering of zombies, and even some ghosts trapped in paintings (including one who had lost his head during the French Revolution).

All followed Hun-Ga-Re's command. "Destroy the Ninjas! Save my bride!!!"

The tomb became the sight of the most unlikely battle of all time! Mummy faced off against robot! Ninja sword clashed against medieval mace. It was total chaos! Dexter, B.O.A.R.D., and the Pink Lynx could only watch helplessly.

As the battle raged, robot limbs and mummy parts flew left and right. A severed ninja arm holding a sword spiraled toward Dex and Aya. It sliced through the rope that bound them to the column.

"We're free!" Dexter cried. "Now let's go get that hoagie!"

"Blip!" B.O.A.R.D. agreed.

Nearby, a certain archvillain watched as his army of N.E.R.T.s was ripped to pieces by the undead.

*This is an unfair fight*, thought Madstachio. When a mummy was punched through the bandages, he kept on going. But when a robot ninja was punched through the circuit board . . . say *sayonara*, Mr. Roboto!

Sensing defeat, Madstachio dashed for the temple's exit, hoagie in hand. He'd get the sandwich back to his lair, then find a way to soften the bread enough to eat it. And anyone who'd ever stood in his way would be sorry!

"He's getting away!" Aya called to Dex and B.O.A.R.D.

A sea of fighting N.E.R.T.s and mummies stood between them and Madstachio.

"Not if I have anything to say about it!" Dex dropped to one knee and took careful aim with his glue pads, knowing that he had only one shot to keep Madstachio from escaping with the hoagie. "Remember your training," he whispered to himself as he hit the trigger.

Madstachio was just steps away from the temple door when a big blob of glue hit him squarely in the face.

Another blob encased his hand, knocking loose the Hoagie of Hun-Ga-Re!

The team watched as the hoagie flew through the air in slow motion.

Dexter knew there wasn't a moment to spare. Without a word, he grabbed the Pink Lynx and jumped on B.O.A.R.D.

"Go, boy! **GO!**" he yelled.

    B.O.A.R.D. didn't need to be told twice. Twin rocket pro-
pulsion units popped out of his deck, and with a roar like a
jet engine, the three shot forward at supersonic speed.

    Dex steered as the Pink Lynx stretched out her cat
claws, and together the team plucked the hoagie out of the
air. Finally, the cursed sandwich was safe!

When they'd landed, Dex took a good look around the temple. The once-evil robot ninjas were evil no longer. Now they just seemed like a harmless junkyard of metal parts. The undead milled about aimlessly without any orders.

Dex spied one last unbroken N.E.R.T. prying Madstachio from the museum tiles. Then he hefted him over his shoulder and slipped through an exit door, carrying his master to safety.

*There's no point in chasing him*, thought Dex. After all, the mission wasn't to capture Madstachio, it was to keep the hoagie safe. And they had succeeded.

Aya looked down sadly at the hoagie. "Dexter, you acted honorably. I was selfish . . . and mean."

"Friends are supposed to forgive each other, right?" Dex held out his hand to shake. "Apology accepted."

The Pink Lynx shook his hand vigorously. "Yes . . . friends!" She smiled behind her cat mask.

129

Meanwhile, Hun-Ga-Re gathered the still-wrapped Millicent in his arms. She yelled from beneath her bandages, "**MMMM! MMMM!**"

"I think we should leave her to the mummy," said Aya with a giggle.

Dex laughed. "We can't do that and you know it. Principal Pickles will never let us go on another field trip if we don't show up together at lunch. Would you mind doing the honors?"

Aya smirked. "Maybe next time." Then she ran at Hun-Ga-Re, leapt through the air, and tore open Millicent's toilet paper casing with one clean swipe of her claws.

Millicent was free! Sort of. She took one look at the giant mummy that held her in his arms and screamed at the top of her lungs. "**YAH! LEMME GO, YOU BIG LUG!**"

Hun-Ga-Re panicked, dropped her, and went and hid in a corner. Millicent didn't stop to thank Dex or Aya before sprinting off to find Principal Pickles.

Aya patted Hun-Ga-Re gently on the shoulder and handed him the hoagie.

"HUN-GA-RE," he said thankfully. Then the giant mummy stomped slowly back to his sarcophagus. Even after a thousand years of rest, he felt pretty beat from the day's activities. He could probably use a good, hundred-year nap. The other undead followed him out of the temple.

Dex couldn't believe it. He looked at Aya. "After all that, you just GAVE it back to him?"

She shrugged. "It's been his for a thousand years now. It just seemed right. I think the secret leaders of the Spectrum of the Cat will understand—and I'm sure the Super-Secret Spy Kids will, too."

Just then, B.O.A.R.D. beeped and the hologram of Big K appeared (regular-size this time). She nodded approvingly. "It was the right thing to do, kid," she said. "We're putting Hun-Ga-Re and the hoagie on the next plane to the Secret Sanctuary of the Spectrum of the Cat. The pharaoh will keep his ancient snack, and the world will still be safe. You may not realize it, Pink Lynx, but the Super-Secret Spy Kids and the Spectrum of the Cat have worked together a number of times in the past."

She gave the Pink Lynx a wink. "In fact, you two make a pretty good team. Let me know if you ever need backup on a mission. Sometimes going solo is best, but sometimes . . ."

Aya smiled. "Sometimes you need help from a friend," she said. "The Spectrum of the Cats thanks you, Big K. And you, B.O.A.R.D. And especially you, Agent SK8. I couldn't have completed the mission without you." She kissed Dex quickly on the cheek. Dex turned beet red. Then the Pink Lynx ran off to supervise the mummy and the cursed hoagie on their journey.

"Ooohh," teased Big K. "Looks like someone's got a little competition for favorite partner, eh, B.O.A.R.D.?" She cleared her throat. "But the important thing is that we kept that hoagie from the clutches of Madstachio!"

"Did you know he was the one who gave me the gamma broccoli?" asked Mr. McFur, who had crowded into the hologram with Big K.

"Bleep blip!" answered B.O.A.R.D.

"He's also our missing inventor, Super-Secret Scientist M!" said Dex.

Big K shrugged. "He doesn't *look* much like our old scientist." She rubbed her chin. "But then again, M didn't have a mustache or an ancient Egyptian headdress. He *did* have very big, very far-out ideas, though."

Dex looked serious. "I have a sneaking suspicion that we'll hear from Madstachio again."

Suddenly, a television monitor lifted out of the pile of broken robot ninja parts. A blurry image of Madstachio appeared on it, his headdress askew and his face still coated in glue.

"You may have won the day, Agent SK8. But I promise you haven't heard the last of MADSTACHIO!" he bellowed. "Oh, and while you're in the museum, go check out those Babylonian plant hangers. *Stunning*, I tell you!" Then the screen went dead.

Everyone looked at Dex.

"Well, obviously, I didn't think that we'd hear from him *immediately*," he said sheepishly.

**AWKWARD, DEX!**
**LUCKY FOR YOU, THE MISSION'S DONE**
**AND WE'VE REACHED**

# THE END!

# GLOSSARY

 **ankh**—a looped cross that was a symbol of life in ancient Egypt

**archaeologist**—a scientist who learns about the past by digging up old objects

**Babylon**—a city in ancient Mesopotamia

 **hieroglyphics**—writing used by ancient Egyptians made of pictures and symbols

**impressionist art**—a French style of painting from the 1800s that creates the feeling of a scene with light and color

 **lynx**—a medium-size wildcat

**Mesopotamia**—an ancient civilization of the Middle East

**pharaoh**—the title of kings in ancient Egypt

**Pre-Raphaelite art**—an English style of painting from the 1800s that portrays people and nature with bright, realistic detail

**sarcophagus**—a stone coffin

 **scarab**—a charm named for the scarab beetle that was popular in ancient Egypt

# Jay Cooper

has worked as a creative director and designer of magazines, books, apparel, and theatrical advertising for two decades. But a book lover before all else, he's at his happiest when creating and illustrating stories for kids. He lives with his wife and children in Maplewood, New Jersey.

# ACKNOWLEDGMENTS

Thanks to Jenne Abramowitz, Teresa Kietlinski, and Nina Goffi for their endless patience; Tommy Greenwald for lighting the way; Vinny Sainato for taking me under his wing; Jim Hoover and Giuseppe Castellano for their friendship and encouragement; and most of all, Laura Wallis, who puts up with me on a daily basis.

# SUPER-SECRET EPILOGUE!

## (For the *real* fans who stay until after the credits!!!!)

Deep in his hidden lair, Madstachio stroked a series of glass cases lit from within. There were five in total. One of the cases held a small sprig of glowing green broccoli that looked as though it had been chewed, swallowed, and then thrown up. The other four cases were empty. He motioned, and a very dinged-up robot ninja handed Madstachio a single slice of tomato that had slipped from the hoagie during the battle.

Grinning crazily, Madstachio placed it in the second case. "Two down. Three to go! And then all the secrets of the universe will be revealed to me!!!"

# Look for Agent SK8's first exciting mission!

When Dexter catches his science teacher performing a super-secret experiment, his school day goes from boring to bonkers! Mr. McFur's lab rat has turned into a King Kong–size rodent—with a temper to match. And Dex doesn't know it yet, but he's the only person who can save his school from total destruction!